For,

my parents,

my sisters, and the rest of my family

who have supported me through everything I have done in life.

A bit about me:

Hello! My name is Ifechukwu Ejiofor, Ife, for short! I love reading books and, as young as I am, I especially love writing stories – it's my hobby! I hope you enjoy this short book as much as I did writing it! Happy reading!

Character List

Main Characters:

- Eveline Westwood, Eve, for short
- Katerina/Katarina Wilkinson, Kitty, for short
- Sally Green
- Megan Hanlon, Megs, for short
- Luna Chausiku
- Coco Raymond

Enemies:

- Hailey Hudson
- Monique Radar

Teachers:

- Mrs Barrell, headmistress
- Mrs Rulebud, Geography teacher
- Miss Beadle, P.E. teacher
- Doctor David, school doctor
- Mrs Haragon (Matron)
- Mrs Garan, head cook
- Miss Bloomsbar, History teacher
- Mrs Haver, headmistress's PA (personal assistant)
- Miss Montone, administrator
- Ms Davis, English teacher
- Ms Jacobs and Ms Teahole, librarian

Others:

- Aunt Lucinda, Kitty's aunt
- Ava, owner of 'Ava's Goodies'
- Joanne, Coco's mother
- Mike, Coco's father
- Rachel, Joanne's sister, Coco's aunt
- Jane McBarter, classmate

Chapter 1

'Good morning!" Eve squealed as she sat up in bed. "It's Friday, the last day of our trip!" She got up and stood her suitcase up and rolled it out of the room.

Her best friend, Kitty, still lay lazily in bed, until Eve shook her awake.

'Come on, Kitty, it's time you got up!"

Kitty turned over and got up, exclaiming, "Where am I, what am I...?"

"Don't be silly. We're on our last day of residential here at Moroley Avenue and you need to get up and roll your suitcase into the corridor."

Kitty got up and did so, her blanket sweeping the floor behind her.

Soon, Eve and Kitty heard the bell they had been warned about, that signalled that it was time to go. Hastily, they pulled some clothes onto themselves, not removing their pyjamas. Eve rushed out of the building and into the coach that was taking the group back to their beloved boarding school, 'Eveleigh Boarding School for Girls'.

However, Kitty stumbled along as though she was a turtle, and it wasn't a surprise when she was the last to get onto the coach.

"Hurry up and get on Kitty! We're going to be there later than expected!" Mrs Rulebud screeched.

Suddenly, Kitty realised that there would be a 2-hour coach ride, and this meant that she could sleep for the whole journey! She nodded at the driver on the way in, and plonked herself down beside Eve, and immediately, breaking the silence of the coach was a loud snore...

Meanwhile, Eve and her other friends – Sally, Megs, Luna and Coco – ate sweets and drank juice, playing 'Truth or Dare' whilst doing so.

When Eve and Kitty returned to their dormitories, Eve instantly started unpacking, and Kitty eventually decided to as well. Eve tidily stored her things away whilst Kitty threw things into place, knocking other things down. As soon as they had finished, they heaved onto their beds.

"That was such a long journey ride," Eve sighed.

"But at least we're back home, and, best of all, I got a 2-hour sleep!"

"I wonder if the rest have finished unpacking," Eve asked. "Let's go and check on them, Kitty."

Eve and Kitty hurried across the corridor and up the long flight of stairs towards their friends' (Sally and Coco) dorms, although it was against the school rules.

Suddenly, there was a loud scream.

Chapter 2

"What is all this noise for?" Miss Beadle, the PE teacher, bellowed. "Oughtn't you to be getting unpacked from your trip?"

"Miss, miss!" Sally exclaimed. "It's Coco, she's, she's...." she gulped.

There was a pause, as the tension grew.

"Dead!" Sally boomed.

Everyone ran out of their rooms, weeping for poor Coco and waiting to hear the plot behind this. Of course, as excited as some were, they all thought it was murder. Miss Beadle burst into Sally's dorm and looked down at the bone-chilling sight of Coco's body, shivering in fright. Trying to hide her worry, Miss Beadle shooed the girls out of the room, including Sally. She called the teachers, including the headmistress, via her walkie-talkie, and they all immediately raced to where the death had occurred.

"What could have happened?" asked Mrs Kanyela, pacing up and down the room frantically.

"Doctor, doctor!" Miss Beadle screeched.

Doctor David rushed out of his office and to the bedroom. He almost fainted at the sight of Coco's body. He pulled on his blue gloves and opened Coco's mouth. It was purple.

"I'm afraid to say that, just by seeing her mouth, I can tell that the reason for Coco's death is poison – which points to murder! It can't be food poisoning as any food colouring that is purple is illegal here!"

"How are we going to tell her parents?" headmistress Mrs Barrell questioned. She shuddered at the thought of ringing a girl's parents to tell them she was no longer alive.

After that, Doctor David rushed out with beads of sweat about to drool down the front of his face. Teachers began to file out of dorm, Mrs Barrell locking the door.

"Sally, Sally!"

Sally quickly ran up to where the headmistress was stood.

"Now Sally, I would like for you NOT to enter, or even try to enter, this room. I would like you to share a dorm with Eveline Westwood and Katerina Wilkinson." Eve and Kitty were nearby and winced when they heard their full names being spoken.

   "Yes!" Sally whispered. She straightened up and cleared her throat. "I mean, yes, Miss!"

"Yes Mrs Barrell!" Mrs Barrell boomed. She hated it when students did not say her full name.

Sally realised that her suitcase and all her prized possessions had already been dragged out of the door, and she climbed down the stairs and into Eve and Kitty's dorm with the load.

"Welcome to our dorm!" Eve excitedly shouted.

However, Kitty grumped, "Oh, I do hate it when Mrs Barrell says our full names. She gets on my nerves. How does she know everyone's names in the school any -"

Suddenly, there was a loud sound outside of the dormitory. Trembling, Sally opened the door. She did not want any more frights – or deaths – to happen. Luckily, it was just Miss Beadle with a bed stand and a mattress.

"Well, don't just stand there watching me. Let me in so I can set this bed up for you."

At hearing this, Sally opened the door wide: what she really needed was a long lie-down on a bed. She had already come back on a 2-hour coach journey and experienced seeing a dead body of one of her best friends. She was devastated.

As soon as Miss Beadle had set the bed stand and mattress up, and Eve, Kitty and Sally had all thanked the PE teacher, Sally plonked herself down on her bed heavily and dozed off into what you could call a long snooze...

After a short while, the bell went for dinner. "Dinner time! Let's go," Kitty said. Eve and Kitty saw how deeply Sally was sleeping and decided to leave her alone. They brought a small plastic bag and decided that they would sneak some food up to their dorm for when she eventually woke up.

At the dining hall, hundreds of girls swarmed around looking for seats with their friends, and, amongst the entire crowd, Eve and Kitty spotted their worst enemy, Hailey Hudson and her snobbish friend, Monique Radar. She was crowded by her gang: they were all gazing in awe at Hailey, as if she was wearing designer wear, making Kitty and Eve feel terribly uncomfortable. How could they think that Hailey was so awesome?

Kitty and Eve queued up for several minutes before they finally got their serving of mashed potatoes, peas and chips. Their school did not believe that girls of their age should be fed any kind of meat or fish.

The pair sat at a table with their friends Megan and Luna, and ate their meal gratefully, happy to be back to Eveleigh school food, and no longer Moroley Avenue's horrid gruel.

When they had almost finished their dinner, they hid some chips inside the bag they had brought along and waved goodbye to their friends. They raced out of the deafening hall and into their calm dorm.

Chapter 3

Surprisingly, Sally was awake and was sat down on one of the chairs doing her homework.

'Sally, we brought some chips for you. I know we aren't allowed, but you need something to eat, right?"

"Do I? I would love anything – even the gruel from Moroley Avenue – to enter my mouth right now!" Sally said, as a loud rumble from her stomach emerged.

Eve and Kitty handed over the chips, and as Sally munched away gratefully, Eve and Kitty reluctantly got their homework out and began to do it. Just then, there was a knock on the door. Kitty opened it, and Matron (Mrs Haragon) stepped inside. Not realising Matron was in the dorm, Sally continued eating her greasy chips.

"Young lady, what are you doing eating chips in a dormitory? How dare you! That will be your first warning!"

Sally hid the chips under her bed and stared down at the floor, scowling at herself. She wondered how she could get so carried away.

"Wretched, old Matron, I'm surprised she didn't snatch the bag of chips off me! I can't wait to finally get out of her grasp when we graduate!" Sally scowled.

Immediately, Sally opened her bed and resumed eating her salty chips. They were nice and crisp, and although they may have been a day or two off, Sally still ate with great contentment.

Meanwhile, Eve had stopped doing her homework, and was now pondering about what the next steps to the investigation of Coco's death could be.

"What on earth will Coco's parents feel like when they get a phone call? I would probably faint if I ever got a phone call giving the message that my daughter was dead!"

"Chill, Eve," Kitty reassured, "I'm sure Mrs Barrell has this under control. We can go and ask tomorrow: after all, we are Coco's friends."

Kitty strolled over to her bed and opened her trunk slightly. She paused as if she didn't know what to expect. It was full to the brim with sweets and chocolates and cakes, looking so tempting and appetising that, as soon as Kitty opened it more widely, her mouth was hanging open.

She took a bag of sweets, and went around the room, handing some out to each of her friends. Then she retreated to her own bed and scoffed all the remaining sweets in her hand.

As she lunged forward to get some more, there was a quiet knock at the door. And what with all the catastrophe and surprises that day, Kitty still dared to stride right up to the door and open it wide. Sally eyes were as wide as saucers.

Luckily, Megan and Luna were waiting outside. "Come on in," Kitty said. One after the other, Megan and Luna stepped inside.

"We were just sharing around some sweets: not that you were going to get any!"

Megan and Luna just stared.

"Kidding!"

Kitty handed a pile of sweets and chocolates out to the girls, and they both nodded in contentment as they munched hard on the tasty treats. Megan and Luna stayed for a while, and they all chatted about seeing Mrs Barrell about the further steps of Coco's death.

"Treat it like we are detectives!" Luna sniggered, though she was only joking.

All the girls laughed uproariously, and then abruptly stopped. They all knew that they shouldn't have taken the death of one of their closest friends as a joke.

"Let's go, before we get caught here."

Megan and Luna got up to leave and silently tip-toed towards the door.

"Ta-ta! See you tomorrow!"

And with that, they left.

"We should be getting to bed too, you know," Kitty sighed.

The threesome got tucked up in bed and immediately fell asleep. They were so worn out after thinking endlessly about Coco. Little did they know that there would be more in store for them the next day.

Next morning, Sally and Eve got up and got showered and dressed. Meanwhile, Kitty, being Kitty, was still snoozing in her bed, dribble oozing uncomfortably out of her mouth.

"Kitty get up! It's Saturday, and it's such a bright day! We can go to the tuck shop," Eve squealed.

At hearing this, Kitty jumped out of her bed and showered quickly and got dressed. She dressed into some old, grey jogging bottoms and a plain, blue top.

"Could you have dressed any more casually?" Sally sighed.

Sally and Eve were in their best dresses as they sashayed up and down the room, giggling as they did so. Kitty just rolled her eyes and beckoned the laughing lunatics to the door.

he three walked down to breakfast. It wasn't as noisy as other days, as people were having a lie-in. All you could here was the clanking of plates. They had jam toast or buttered toast as an option.

"Only one slice each! If you come late, you get what the late-comers deserve!" screeched Mrs Garan, the head chef.

"Thanks, Kitty," Eve said sarcastically, as she grabbed a piece of buttered toast.

Kitty rolled her eyes again, sneakily grabbed two pieces of toast and jam when Mrs Garan wasn't watching and sat down at the table where Megan and Luna were sat.

Eve and Sally came and sat down where the others were sat too, and Megan and Luna were astonished at how appropriately they had dressed.

"What's the big occasion?" Luna asked, biting her lip.

"Oh, we forgot to say. We were planning to go to the tuck shop. Do you want to come?"

"Do I?" Luna said. "Yes, yes, yes! Come on, Megs. Let's go and get ready!"

Luna dragged Megs off to their dorm and they both immediately got dressed.

Worriedly, Eve, Kitty and Sally sneaked over to Megs and Luna's dorm on the second floor. They gently knocked, and, unexpectedly, the door opened swiftly.

"Come on in! We are almost ready," Megs said.

Eve, Kitty and Sally entered the tidy room. Kitty gazed in awe at how neat the room appeared to be, and Luna laughed hysterically.

"You've just got to live in the room with a girl who loves cleanliness," Luna said, staring at Megs and shaking her head.

Megs and Luna were in their best dresses, and they brought their mini purses along.

"Let's go!" Megs squealed.

All five girls hurried out of the room, raced downstairs, and stormed out of the door. They were so glad to, at last, get some fresh air. Bunches of other girls were scattered around the town of Eveleigh and were heading in different directions to their favourite tuck shops.

The girls' favourite tuck shop was 'Ava's Goodies', and they weren't changing their mind today. They headed straight on, Luna leading the way. On the way, Eve couldn't help but bring up the question that they had all been asking themselves.

"How on earth did Coco die? I overheard Doctor Death say it was murder," Eve asked.

Luna's eyes widened.

"Who would have murdered her? I ask you, who murdered my friend?"

The fearsome five arrived at 'Ava's Goodies' and opened the door that had a bell ring after it.

"Hi, girls! It's so nice to have you back. Business has been bad recently."

"Hi, Ava! Just feeling like getting a few snacks each, as it's so bright today!"

The girls all managed to squeeze into different aisles, grabbing as many sweets as they wanted. When they had finished, they went to get a pick and mix. They all just managed to finish up before the shop closed.

As Ava collected the money for all their goodies, she counted how many girls there were.

"One, two, three, four, ...five? Where's Coco?"

The girls shuffled around uncomfortably, looking for a way to explain that Coco was dead.

"You see," Kitty began, "Coco, she... died."

Ava's eyes widened. She stopped, apologised for bringing it up, and waved goodbye pitifully.

"Sorry about Coco's death. I hope you find out the reason for it."

The girls walked off, silent as they did so. Breaking the silence, Sally asked, "Should we go to 'Carnivals?'"

"Sure, whatever," came Megs' grumpy reply.

'Carnivals' was a café, one of the girls' favourites, where they would usually go and get lunch on a Saturday. The five walked in slowly and ordered their food. Eve and Sally got mashed potatoes and curry, whilst Megs and Luna ordered two slices of pizza.

Kitty, however, was singled out with no money.

"Come on Kitty, how about me and Megs put our money together, remove our orders, and put a new one in for a large pizza?" Luna said.

"No, no, don't worry about it. You keep your money for next week. My Aunt Lucinda will send me some more on Thursday."

Megs, Luna, Eve and Sally sat at a table together and ate their dishes quickly, whilst Kitty stood around waiting for them. Sally had asked her to take a seat, but she rejected it.

Soon enough, the girls had gobbled all their food. They grabbed their bags and pick and mix pots, and off they were, back to school, where everything would be safe and sound.

Or so they thought.

Chapter 4

As the five filed back into school, all they could here around them was chatter about Coco's death. The news had spread like a virus; even as they all returned to Megan and Luna's dorm, there was still a sense that the girls' thoughts were being read out aloud.

Luna slammed the door behind them, and the other four shook violently and stared.

"What?" she questioned, laughing nervously.

"Well, I am glad my thoughts aren't literally being read out loud by other people," Eve sighed sarcastically.

"Oh, we almost forgot," Sally said, "we have to go and ask Mrs Barrell for further information about how you-know-who died, and how it's being dealt with."

"Well, what are we waiting for? Let's go!"

The five escaped from the room once again, to hear the non-stop rumours about Coco. The news had travelled at the speed of light!

After trekking up eight staircases, the girls had finally made it outside a door holding a sign that said, 'Mrs Barrell – Knock and enter by appointment only.'

"Sorry, but we have no time to make an appointment. This is a matter of urgency."

And, with that, Kitty barged the door open, terrifying a flustered-looking Mrs Barrell.

"How dare you enter without knocking or appointment, Katarina! I shall have to report this to your parents!"

"Sorry for the mistake, Mrs Barrell, but this is an emergency! As you know, our friend, Coco, has passed away, and, to sum it up, we want to know what the plan is for finding out who the murderer is!" Eve finished, worn out from speaking for so long so quickly.

"Eveline! No need to get so worked up! Since, and only since, you were her closest friends, I will let you in on what the next steps are. But let this be a warning to you – what is said in these walls, stays in these walls. Understood?" the headmistress said.

"Yes Mrs Barrell," the five chanted.

"So, I had an extremely upsetting phone call with Coco's parents, Joanne and Sam, and they were so heartbroken that I could hear the sorrow in their voices. The couple are coming to collect her on Tuesday morning. I phoned up the police and they will come and investigate her body tomorrow, as well as questioning everyone who went on the trip, and a few teachers," Mrs Barrell explained.

"So, it really is murder!" Luna muttered under her breath.

At this point in time, tears were crawling out of Megs', Eve's and Sally's eyes. Kitty and Luna were just too strong to cry and thought of it as 'a baby's thing'.

"Thank you so much for updating us!" Luna said, and the five filed out of the door, shutting it quietly behind them.

"I guess we just have to wait for the police to arrive tomorrow," Sally sighed.

Megs and Luna went back to their dorm, and Eve, Kitty and Sally also returned to their own. They all put their purses away, and sat down on the floor in a circle, eating the sweets they had bought earlier.

"I didn't even get to say goodbye to Coco!" Kitty exclaimed.

"No one did," Sally said sadly.

"Let's go to the library, we definitely need a break after all of this mess," Eve said.

The three headed off to the school library. It was in the basement, the most horrifying part of the school. It was covered in spiders' webs and covered in black blankets to hide the wallpaper that was peeling off. When the girls made their way through with their textbooks and homework, they were worn out. They sat down at the huge hexagonal table that they always sat at and began their remaining homework.

Curiously, Kitty looked through the thousands of ancient books and spotted a book about murder, and reasons for murder. She asked the librarian if she could borrow it, and as Ms Teahole scanned the book, she looked petrified. She couldn't believe that a girl of Kitty's age would want to read such a book.

When the book had finished being scanned through, Kitty took it and sat back down at the same table. She opened to the first few pages, past the credits, until she got to the contents.

"Guys, I borrowed a book about murder," Kitty said. "And I also overheard Doctor David say her mouth was purple.

The pair was too driven into their homework to bother about what Kitty was saying. Still, Kitty looked up and down for 'purple mouth murder' but couldn't find it. She gave up looking, and instead nudged Sally.

"Sally, I need your help. As I just said, I overheard Doctor David say that Coco's mouth was purple, but I have looked for 'purple mouth murder' here, and I can't find it. I was hoping you might know?"

"Oh, Kitty," Sally said. "Why didn't you ask before? Coco's purple mouth means that there must have been murder through poisoning, as, I myself, know that purple food-colouring in food is illegal – plus Coco hates the colour purple."

"So, am I looking for poison, then?" Kitty questioned, getting desperate.

"Yes, Kitty, yes you are," Sally replied.

Kitty skimmed through the contents again, and, soon enough, there it was – 'Murder through Poisoning'. Kitty could also see that the writing was slightly smudged and vaguely underlined. She didn't take it as a suspicion, and just as she was about to open the book, the dinner bell went.

Time had flown by so quickly! The girls rushed through the spiders' webs and up the creaky, wooden stairs back to their dorm, where they dropped their books and ran to the dinner hall.

"You're just in time for beans and sausages, ladies!" Mrs Garan screeched. The girls collected their meals and headed to a table. Megs and Luna came in much later than usual and joined them at the same table.

"Sorry we were late," Luna gasped, trying to hold herself together. "We sat eating the sweets we'd bought, and then we counted how much money we had left in our purses. We finally started taking off our dresses and mine got stuck, so Megs had to help me. It took forever! I'm flustered!"

"Sorry about that Luna," Sally said pitifully.

"Guess what I borrowed from the library?" Kitty said excitedly.

"WHAT?" Megs and Luna asked.

"A book, about murder. Yes, that's right, and I found a page about poison, because of what happened to Coco."

"Cool, me and Luna can come to your dormitory to discover more," Megs said, coolly.

The girls munched their food hastily, scraped their plates, and headed straight for Eve and Kitty's dorm. Just as the girls arrived, they all stopped in their tracks, stood still, and stared in horror. There, standing outside the door was Matron.

And she looked very unpleased.

"Going somewhere?" she said.

"We...err...we," Eve stuttered.

"Enough with the stuttering, young lady. This room is in an ugly mess! I shall have to report you to your head of year, though he never does anything about it! I've heard that you

have already had a report to your parents, Kitty Wilkinson."

"How did she know?" Kitty murmured under her breath. Luna gave an empathetic look and dragged Megs off to their dorm, before they got caught up in Matron's tangle.

Meanwhile, Matron was fuming.

"Clean that room immediately!"

"Yes, Matron!" the girls chorused.

The three stormed into the dorm and slammed the door shut. They hastily went around the room cleaning and tidying things away; in their haste, they stumbled a lot. Eventually, it was looking as neat as Megs and Luna's room - almost.

Tired out, they changed into their pyjamas as fast as they could, before they dropped down to the floor with sleepiness.

Chapter 5

After prayer time and plenty of rest on Sunday, the following morning, there was a deafening knock at the front entrance. A booming voice followed.

"We're here, open up!" a policeman shouted.

The receptionist let the pair of policemen into the boarding school, and they took a seat, waiting for the headmistress.

However, on the other side of the school, Eve, Kitty and Sally were pulling themselves out of bed and showering and dressing. They managed to get themselves ready just before the bell went for breakfast. Breakfast was early on weekdays, and the girls knew that they needed to hurry if they even wanted a chance of grabbing a spoon.

Weekdays meant lumpy porridge for breakfast, but today, there was not one lump in sight!

"Hah! Maybe it's because the canteen staff thought policemen were coming in here!"

Mrs Garan overheard this, and, realising the policemen weren't in school just to look at porridge, she went into a rage.

"Oh, don't worry, Mrs Garan. I love the way you've made the porridge with not a single lump in sight!" Kitty reassured, slyly.

"Don't be so cheeky!" Mrs Garan yelled.

It had turned out that half of Kitty's year group was waiting impatiently for their porridge to be served, including Megs and Luna. Irritated, Eve and Sally dragged Kitty to a table with the bowls of porridge.

"Wow, Kitty! You held everyone back. Everyone was staring at you, and they all looked like they couldn't wait to eat! Look, now, our food is getting cold!" Eve complained.

The three instantly gobbled their food up. Megs and Luna came to join them and ranted at Kitty jokingly. Soon enough, the bell went for end of breakfast, and the girls speedily ran to their dorms to collect their books.

The first two lessons were History and English, two subjects that Sally absolutely hated. Eve and Kitty managed to grab hold of their textbooks, but Sally had to go on a hunt in the room to find hers.

"Come on, Sally," Kitty moaned. "We need to go now or else we'll be late!"

"I'll just have to tell Mrs Bloomsbar that I can't find my History book," Sally sighed. "Oh!" she lightened up. "At least I've found my English book. Phew, Ms Davis won't yell at me."

"Let's just go," said Eve restlessly.

The three headed off to the other building, Graghall, where all the lessons – for all the girls – were located. As you can imagine, the building was very big. Every year, they had to extend it, because more Year 7 girls than expected joined the school, as well as exchange students.

History was their first lesson, but they had forgotten that the police were coming to the school. The lesson started at nine o'clock and ran as normal (apart from the fact that Sally hadn't found her textbook and got a shouting-at from Miss Bloomsbar), right until there was a knock at the door.

The history teacher shouted, "Come in!"

At once, the policemen strode through the doorway. Miss Bloomsbar looked slightly astonished and flushed, as well as ashamed of herself for allowing the policemen to come in so informally.

"We are here to see all those girls who went on the trip to..."

He looked down at his sheet of paper, cleared his throat, and then looked up.

"Moroley Avenue?"

Almost all the class stood up. The only people left sitting down were Hailey Hudson and Monique Radar. Their parents were fuming with their grades and had refused to pay for the trip.

"One at a time, ladies, one at a time," the other policeman cautioned. "We will take you out in pairs, so we don't miss a spot of vital information, because, I promise you, we will find out who this murderer is."

The other policeman continued, "The closest friends of Coco Raymond – that's Eve, Sally, Megan, Luna and Kitty – will be interviewed as a group. This will all be carried out during this lesson. Is that OK, Miss Bloomsbar?"

Miss Bloomsbar looked as red as a tomato, but to redeem herself from before, she nodded her head, pursed her lips, and turned to her computer.

"Perfect, can I take Emma and Ava, please?" the policeman politely asked.

Emma and Ava stepped forward and out of the door, where all there was to hear was a faint murmuring sound. Eve, Sally, Megs, Luna and Kitty were biting their lips and looking frantically round at each other.

Kitty mouthed, "At least we'll be with each other."

In and out of doors, in and out of doors, and finally, it was the girls' turn. They all stepped outside, not saying a word.

"Now, I know you were the closest to Coco Raymond, so

I know just how you will be feeling that she has now passed away, but I just need to ask you few questions before her parents come and take her body away tomorrow."

"So," the other policeman began, "Do you know of anything Coco may have eaten?"

The girls racked through their brains, but they knew Coco well, and she never bought anything when they went to the tuck shop: and she never let anyone give her anything they had bought.

"All she ate was school meals, breakfast, lunch and dinner," Eve replied.

"Ok, thank you," the policeman said. He scribbled a few notes down in his notepad.

"Have any of you ever had a terrible argument with Coco, making you want to have revenge on her?"

This question was useless to the girls. Of course, they hadn't had reason to argue with Coco! She was their best friend!

"Not at all!" Luna said, a tone of surprise in her voice.

The policeman scribbled more notes down, and Kitty impolitely peered over to try and see what he was writing.

"And one last question for Sally," the policeman said.

"Did Coco make any strange movements or signs of worsening health whilst you were unpacking from your trip?"

Sally thought for a moment, and then answered, "Her health was in good state from the time we came back up until she died. She was just the normal best friend I'd always known!"

The policeman scribbled down his final notes to the girls and said, "Thank you."

Just as he said so, the bell rang for end of the first lesson. The girls grabbed their books and headed onto their next lesson, English. In English, they were studying the book, 'A Midsummer Night's Dream', a book that Sally did not understand one little bit.

"Shakespeare's language is so bizarre," she said.

The lesson ran as normal, with Sally staring out of the window and not paying attention. She was thinking about the next two lessons, her favourites, Science and Maths. When the bell rang, Sally was delighted as she let her daydream slip away. She rushed straight to the dining room to get a protein bar, as a reward for not going into a rant about History and English.

However, Hailey stopped her in her tracks.

"What are you doing here, Silly?" she sneered.

Sally hated it when Hailey made fun of her name and turned it from Sally to silly.

"Don't call me that!" she shouted.

"Aww, little Silly's getting angry now, is she? As I asked, what *are* you doing here? Aren't you too poor to even afford a slice of toast, let alone get another snack at break time for your greedy little self?"

Sally just ignored her and bought herself a protein bar. She knew her family weren't as rich as Hailey's, but that didn't mean that she had to be called 'poor'. She ran off in tears to the dormitory but wiped them away when she arrived.

Chapter 6

After three more lessons, the school day was finally over. Megs, Luna, Eve, Kitty and Sally went to book an appointment to meet with Mrs Barrell, regarding what the police had reported back.

"What time are you looking at, girls?" Mrs Barrell's PA, Mrs Haver, asked sweetly.

"Maybe after dinner, around six-thirty?" Luna asked.

"Yes, of course. There you go, six o'clock." Mrs Haver handed a pass to Megs, as evidence that they had really booked a meeting. The girls left Mrs Haver's office, and then suddenly remembered that they had been given homework for the next day in Maths.

"Oh no! Remember the maths homework we need to submit tomorrow?" Eve said.

"Oh, yeah," Kitty replied. "Let's grab our textbooks and got to the library."

The girls hurried to their dorms, snatched their books off their beds, without looking back, and rushed through the cobwebs to the library. They all sat down at the hexagonal table and jotted down the answers in urgent haste to get down to dinner early.

When they had finished, they sighed deeply and rushed off, just as the bell rang for dinner. They got to the dining hall ten seconds after the bell and were given the best serving of pasta and pesto ever.

Aware of how much time they had until their meeting with Mrs Barrell, the girls did not talk to each other at all, and they finished their meals quickly. The five returned to their dorms and rested for a while before realising that it was six twenty-five.

"Time to go!" Kitty exclaimed. "Let's go and get Megs and Luna!"

Just as Kitty was saying this, Megs and Luna knocked, and Kitty opened the door.

"We were just about to get you, but no need! Let's go!"

The five headed downstairs and, soon enough, they were standing outside the headmistress's office.

"Please don't let Kitty knock this time," Eve pleaded. "The headmistress is tired as it is."

Instead, Luna knocked very gently, but so that Mrs Barrell was still able to hear.

"Come in!" she said.

The girls entered quietly and sat down, as the headmistress had told them to take a seat.

"So, girls," Mrs Barrell said. "Why have you come to meet with me?"

"Well," Luna began. "We were wondering if, perhaps, the police had given feedback on the investigation."

"Oh, honestly, girls," the headmistress said, "You really do care for Coco, don't you?"

"Yes, of course!" Eve spluttered, then, humiliated, shut her mouth.

"Like I said in the last meeting, do not tell anybody that I am giving you the information and don't tell anybody the information. Got it?"

"Got it," the girls chorused.

"Ok, the police have said that, unfortunately, they do not see a reason why Coco could have been murdered by anyone in this school. They went to check her body and her purple mouth, but, even if it was murder, the police can't do anything about it, because whoever targeted her as the victim is, according to the policemen's notes, out of school," the headmistress finished.

The girls sighed in dismay. There was nothing they could do before they waved bye-bye to Coco the next day. Suddenly, Kitty had a brilliant idea.

She said sympathetically, "Mrs Barrell, after all of our sorrows for Coco, we don't even get to say goodbye! What I am asking is if we can please go into the room with Coco's parents – they'll be fine with us as they know us very well – and see Coco before she goes."

The other four girls hopefully looked up, their pleading eyes making Mrs Barrell to consider what Kitty had said.

"Oh, alright then," she finally said. "But behave and do as everyone asks you to. I myself would like for you not to touch her body at all."

The girls tried their best to hide their horror. Coco had been their friend, but that didn't mean they had to touch a dead body to say goodbye.

The five thanked Mrs Barrell and headed out of the door.

"That last bit gave me the shivers," Eve whispered to Sally.

Sally nodded understandingly and gave Eve a pat on the shoulder.

Just as they were about to climb up the stairs to bed, Mrs Barrell stuck her head out of her door and said, "I forgot! Since you girls are so grieved, I am giving you special permission to go to each other's dorms, but no one else's!"

The girls whooped quietly with joy and headed up the stairs, jumping with glee.

"Let's go to Eve and Kitty's dorm and have a sleepover. There are more beds."

So, the girls rushed up, brushed their teeth and changed into their pyjamas. Megs and Luna had to sneak past Matron's room and into their own, to get their pillows, and anything else they needed. They rushed back and slept at the other end of Eve and Sally's bed.

Kitty was a rough sleeper, so no one wanted to sleep at the other end of *her* bed.

"So, is there absolutely nothing *we* can do?" Eve asked. Suddenly, she remembered how Luna had joked about being detectives.

"Luna, remember how you joked about us being detectives? Don't you think we should find out who murdered Coco? I personally think that it's someone in the school."

"Eve, don't be silly," Luna said, "we can't, can we?"

"Yes! Why didn't I think of that? Let's do it," Kitty said.

"So, we can have our meetings every Tuesday, Thursday and Friday."

"Ok. I'm getting tired. Goodnight, everyone," Luna said.

"Goodnight," the rest said.

Eve turned out the lights and the girls slowly drifted off to sleep, having nightmares about what Mrs Barrell had said about not touching Coco's body.

Chapter 7

The next day, as the girls were getting ready for breakfast, Coco's parents, Joanne and Mike, were waiting at the front entrance for them to be let through. Joanne walked up to the administrator, Miss Montone.

"How long will we be waiting for?" she asked politely. "We need to collect Coco as we have things to be doing."

"Not long now," Miss Montone replied. "I am just waiting for the headmistress to come and take you to Coco –."

Mrs Barrell unexpectedly walked through the doors and greeted Joanne and Mike. She led them through the double doors and up two flights upstairs, until they got to Coco's room.

The headmistress searched her pockets until she found the keys to the room. Joanne gasped as she unlocked it. A foul smell emerged as the three entered.

Meanwhile, Eve, Kitty and Sally were sat in the dining hall, eating the original, lumpy porridge. When they had finished, they rushed down to their first lesson, French, and made it just in time for the register.

"Good morning Eve," the teacher said.

"Good morning Madame Duval," Eve said, sitting down.

After fifteen minutes of the lesson, Eve, Kitty, Sally, Luna and Megs were called out of the classroom by Mrs Barrell. Everybody stared – Hailey and Monique staring enviously – at the girls as they walked out with their books. No one else knew that they were about to witness a dead body.

Mrs Barrell took them up to the dorm they all knew, and, gulping because of the reek, the girls entered. Megs and Sally waved at Mike, and he nodded calmly back.

"Yesterday, the police interviewed everyone who went on the trip. They couldn't find any reason why she would be murdered by somebody in this school. So, they said they can't do any further investigation," Mrs Barrell.

"Thank you, Mrs Barrell. All that matters is that, now, she will be with us."

All the girls starting weeping, knowing that Coco would no longer with them. Luna and Kitty tried to hold back their tears, but they just couldn't do it. Even as disgusting as Coco's body was, they all wanted to hold her hand and say goodbye at this moment. However, they had remembered what Mrs Barrell had said about not touching the body, and instead, they just kept weeping and weeping. It was a heart-breaking moment for Joanne, Mike and Mrs Barrell.

"You girls will be dehydrated by the time you are done with all of this crying," Mrs Barrell said, sadly. "After this, you can get a drink of water before you go back to lessons."

"Yes, Mrs Barrell," the girls replied in muffled voices. They quickly wiped their tears away, before they dried, and continued to look down at their best friend's body.

Joanne had called her sister to come down with her Range Rover to come and collect Coco in a separate car, but she hadn't arrived yet.

Suddenly, Joanne's phone beeped. "Hello?"

"Hi, Joanne, this is Rachel," she said. "I am here with the car for Coco."

"Great, thanks, we'll meet you outside the front entrance. You've done us a huge favour. Thanks once again. Bye!"

The headmistress went and got the caretakers to lift the body down the stairs and out of the front entrance, into the car. The girls came with them to say goodbye once again, and, on behalf of Coco, they said that Joanne and Mike were the best parents ever. This melted their hearts.

"And, on behalf of Coco," Mike said. "You are the best friends I could ever have."

The girls were given cups of water before returning to lessons. They had missed the whole of the second and third lesson, as well as break, so they only had two more lessons left to go until the end of the school day. They returned to English with their books and made it just in time to continue reading 'A Midsummer Night's Dream.'

All the girls stared at their entry into the classroom.

"And what made you girls so late?" Ms Davis said.

"We went to see Coco, headmistress's orders," Kitty said.

The girls took their seats and read silently, though their minds weren't focused on what they were reading. It was what they had just been through that their minds were focused on.

Chapter 8

After the school day was finished, the girls were staggering as they made their way to Megs and Luna's dorm.

When they entered and had shut the door, Eve said, "We have to get to the bottom of this. We aren't getting enough sleep because of this murder, so we may as well resolve it. Yes, I know this is a murder that has been carried out by someone in school, because Coco is never exposed to anyone outside of school who isn't related to her."

"I don't care which days we have these meetings," Luna said, "As long as everyone's free."

"Oh, I remember! I borrowed a library book about murders. Should I go and get it?" Kitty asked.

"Yes! But be careful: Matron lurks around here at this time," Megs warned.

Kitty hurried quickly, and, remembering what Megs had said about Matron, she dived into the room and got her murder book that was shoved under her bed. As she was racing out, she met eye-to-eye with Matron.

"Katarina! Where are you heading to? Your dormitory is down there!" Matron sneered.

Kitty was speechless. In fact, she was heading back to Megs and Luna's dorm, but of course she wasn't going to tell Matron the truth, was she? She was about to say that she was heading for the lavatories, but then she had remembered that Mrs Barrell had given the five, special permission, to go to each other's dorms.

"Actually, Matron," Kitty sneered back, "Mrs Barrell gave us five, special permission to go to each other's dormitories, so, thanks very much for asking."

And, with that, Kitty continued going up the stairs, this time with a stride in her step. Matron muttered something under her breath and stumbled off in her slippers.

When Kitty opened the door, the others freaked out and gasped.

"Relax, guys, it's only me," she said. "Sorry I'm so late back. Matron stopped me and asked me why I was going in the direction of your dorm. I told her that Mrs Barrell had given us special permission, and she just grunted and wandered off!"

"It's fine," Luna said. "We were only discussing how this should all be kept a secret, you know, us trying to find out who the mystery murderer is."

"Oh, yeah, sure," Kitty said. "It's like you read my mind, Luna. I was going to mention that."

"Anyway, let's study this book," Megs reminded the others. The girls immediately opened the book and Kitty took the lead in turning to the page where it explained murder by poison."

Luna took a deep breath in as her eyes met with the page.

"I also noticed that, in the contents, the heading saying, 'Murder by Poison' is smudged slightly."

"We have to start making a suspect list," Eve said, tearing a sheet of paper out of Megs' notebook. "If you say that the heading was smudged, Kitty, then this means that it's obviously someone who visits the library a lot, apart from us."

"Are you sure, Eve?" Luna questioned. "It could have been anyone! Everyone has been to the library before, and everyone knows that if you need information like this, you need to go to the library!"

"Ok, I'll consider that as I'm writing the suspect list down."

"So," Sally said. "We can put down our enemies first, like Hailey and Monique – they would definitely have a motive – and then, who do we know who visits the library at least once every three weeks?"

"Oh! Jane McBarter does! I see her heading down there after Science every Wednesday!"

Eve scribbled down Jane's name, as well as how often she visited the library.

"The librarian might," Sally said quietly. "She's always been so mystifying and gloomy.

Eve noted down the librarian down too, as well as her motive.

"That's all for now," Eve said. She slid the sheet of paper inside the murder book. Suddenly, the dinner bell rang.

"Why are we always caught out by the dinner bell?" Luna sighed.

The girls cut their meeting short and went to get some dinner, before the line grew too long. For dinner, it was parsnip and carrot soup, with bread alongside it. The girls didn't exactly savour this atrocious meal; in fact, they would usually shove the soup down the drains when the staff weren't looking and feed the bread to the birds.

This time though, the girls were starving. They grabbed their soup and bread, almost delighted, and drank up the whole thing at once. They munched hard on their bread and finished within a minute.

The girls raced out of the dining hall and into the corridor. It was clear that all of them had noticed that Hailey hadn't come down to dinner, which meant that something was going on.

When Eve, Kitty and Sally went to pick up the murder book from Megs and Luna's dorm, it was nowhere to be found.

"I don't understand!" Kitty exclaimed. "I left it right on the-"

"Looking for this?" Hailey sneered. She was holding the murder book in her hand. The girls had suspected something wrong was going on. "Why would you want to borrow a *murder* book, if you weren't going to murder someone, hm? Still, I can't be bothered investigating any further in this horrifying business, I have better things to be doing! But, watch out!" And, with that, Hailey dropped the book on the floor, rolled her eyes, and sashayed off with a smug expression on her face.

"What is wrong with that girl? I'm going to get her!" Kitty screeched.

"Not too loud, Kitty. Matron's around. I heard a rumour that Matron had moved down to your floor, just to keep an eye on you, Kitty," Megs warned again.

Kitty bent down and picked up the book furiously. Eve and Sally waved goodbye to Megs and Luna and the three headed out and downstairs. They didn't talk until they got into the dorm, scared that Matron would catch them out. It was just a few minutes until lights out, so Eve, Sally and Kitty got dressed whilst eating sweets. The last thing they had to do was brush their teeth in the lavatories upstairs.

"We need to stop eating our sweets after we've brushed," Eve said.

The girls rushed up to the lavatories and brushed their teeth, then got back down and straight into bed.

"I'm surprised Hailey didn't report to Matron, or even Mrs Barrell!" Sally said.

"Well, she said that she had better things to be doing. Kitty, what do you think?" Eve asked.

Kitty didn't answer.

"Kitty?"

A sudden snore erupted out of Kitty, and Sally and Eve giggled quietly for what seemed like forever. They quickly grew weary, and soon fell asleep.

Chapter 9

After school was finished for the week, Saturday morning came around and, surprisingly, Kitty was the first to wake up.

"Guys! I'm way too excited to have breakfast. We must go to 'Ava's Goodies' and tell Ava we're carrying out the investigation!"

"Oh, come on, Kitty! It's too early, breakfast is in two hours! You'll be hungry by then. But, seeing as I'm awake now, I may as well get ready."

Woken by the noise, Sally also woke up and got ready. The three wore jeans and their matching tops and creeped up to Megs and Luna's bedroom to tell them to wear theirs too.

"Why are you waking us up so early? It's only six o'clock!" Luna complained.

Despite this, Luna and Megs showered and dressed into their clothes, and then Kitty told them they should tell Ava about the investigation.

"Are you sure? I thought we agreed it was supposed to stay a secret, and Ava might tell school; you know what she's like. She just can't help herself!" Luna said.

"Luna, she's the only person, apart from ourselves, that we can trust, and if we get into trouble or danger, she can defend us. Don't sweat it," Kitty reassured.

"What we should be thinking about is how we're going to spend one hour in this room until breakfast," Eve said.

"We could go to the library. It always seems to be open," Sally said.

"Let's go then. But, be very quiet. We can't let anyone hear us at this time."

The girls sneakily crept out in their matching outfits and slipped into the library through the cobwebs that had somehow grown.

As guessed, the librarian was sat down reading a book. Sally was right: the library did seem like it was always open! The girls each grabbed a book about murder and sat down to read. Forty-five minutes went and neither of the girls had finished reading their books.

"Well, we just can't borrow them. Ms Jacobs will go crazy if she sees five people borrowing murder books. More than that, she'll think *we* murdered Coco!"

The girls had to leave the books behind and got through the cobwebs and back to Megs and Luna's dorm.

"Are you hungry now, Kitty?" Eve said, nudging Kitty's elbow as they walked.

"Am I? I'm starving!" Kitty exclaimed.

When the girls returned to the dorm, they had only ten minutes before breakfast. Megs and Luna let the others have some of their sweets, and they all munched quietly on them until the bell went. The girls rushed down the stairs, and to their surprise, they were the first ones in the dining hall.

"Whatever made you so early?" Mrs Garan said.

"Oh, aren't we always on time, Miss?" Kitty said slyly.

"Young madam, one more time I catch you being cheeky, you'll be in my lumpy porridge!"

Kitty daringly laughed and the others widened their eyes, but luckily, Mrs Garan didn't hear the giggle. The girls sat down with three slices of toast and ate quickly so that they could leave.

When they had finished, and had put their dishes away, they walked out of the dining hall and into their dorms to get their purses. They strolled back down and out of the front entrance door, and into the street. Some girls had followed behind them, but they were probably just Year 7 girls who wouldn't bother them.

"Where do we properly begin with all of this investigating?" Luna asked.

"I was thinking that we could start writing down suspects," Megs said quietly.

"We could start off with going to *the scene of the crime*!" Kitty roared.

A few people stared at the group, and Eve scolded Kitty jokingly.

"Kitty, lots of people were just staring at you! Do you know how embarrassing that was for us as your friends? One day, I'll pretend I don't even know you!" Eve said, but then laughed at what she had said.

Kitty rolled her eyes and smirked at her best friend. "As if she would even dare to pretend not to know me!" Kitty thought to herself.

The girls walked on talking and contributing their ideas; eventually, Luna just said that Ava could help them. Suddenly, they heard a cackle behind them. The five twirled around to meet their enemy, Monique.

"Oh no, it's a shame I couldn't hear *all* of your brilliant ideas of how to solve the investigation! Yes, I have been listening, and yes, I have been writing notes. You know me, *I* may not be in the popularity zone, but Hailey is. When I show these to her, she'll love me even more! She won't be able to hold her tongue. She'll tell everyone!"

Monique sashayed off, turning around and sticking her tongue out as she did so.

"We're going to be in *so* much trouble if Mrs Barrell finds out. We may even be expelled!" Eve wailed.

"Chill, Eve," Kitty said. "Trying to do the school a favour is most definitely not going to lead to expulsion."

"We just need to ask Ava how to get rid of enemies standing in our way," Sally scolded.

"You know, I don't feel like buying anything after our investigation secret got out to our worst enemies," Megs said. "Still, we should go to Ava."

The others agreed with Megs and so they stormed off to 'Ava's Goodies', irritated.

"Morning girls! How are you all doing?" Ava said, with a shake of nerve in her voice.

"Erm, Ava, we were just going to say –"

"Say no more!" Ava said in a shaky tone as she grabbed all the girls' favourite sweets, splashed them onto the counter and had already started scanning them.

"AVA! LISTEN!" Kitty exclaimed

The girls look in shock at Kitty and Kitty just shrugged her shoulders and put her hands in her pockets.

"So," Kitty continued, "we weren't actually intending to *buy* anything today, we're just all a little frustrated and flustered."

"A little?" Eve sighed grumpily.

"I'll do the explaining," yawned Luna. "We were intending to come and tell you that we were going to try to investigate how Coco was murdered, and see if you would agree with the idea, as well as ideas and tips on how to go about it. We were all discussing our ideas, maybe a little too loud, and then our enemy, Monique, was following us, taking notes, and she's going to expose our plan! I feel like it's all my fault. I was too loud and too eager," Luna finished.

"Wait, wait!" Ava exclaimed, "The girl you mentioned who was following you, what was her name?"

"Monique, Monique Radar," Eve said. "Why?"

"Girls, I should have told you the minute you walked in. You see, Monique came into the shop threatening to tear it down, yesterday late at night, when I was about to close the shop."

"But we're not allowed to go out on weekdays!" Megs and Sally said together.

"Well at least we have something to threaten her if she tries to get us into trouble," Kitty said.

"However, you say you want to investigate this murder. Well, I haven't read many of Robin Stevens' novels, but I know that you need to make a suspect list with a motive under each suspect. Make sure you include yourselves among the list, because you may be accused, but, of course, I know you would never murder Coco. Make sure to borrow books from your library on the topic of murder and-''

"We thought about that, but it would look suspicious if we all borrowed books about murder."

"Then all decide on one book that you think would be best and benefit all of you," Ava continued, "Come on girls, we have to make things work! We'll get nowhere if we don't! I'm counting on you, you know, I know you can do it!"

"Ok, thank you so much Ava!" the girls all gushed. With a feeling of fright slightly lifted off their shoulders, they left the shop.

Chapter 10

After walking for a mile, the girls eventually got to 'Carnivals'. As they slid through the narrow door, a shopkeeper waved to them cheerfully and they waved back and sat down at their seats.

Soon enough, the shopkeeper had taken their orders, and in front of them was a basket of chips each and a bottle of mineral water for Eve, Sally and Megan. Luna and Kitty wanted to spice things up, so they ordered two extra bottles of Sprite instead of water.

Once they had finished, they rushed out, waving goodbye to the shopkeeper in the empty restaurant. The girls almost felt like it was *their* shop, as every Saturday they would go to 'Carnivals' and no one would be there.

As they were walking back to school, exhausted, they noticed huddles of girls swarming the pavements. Luna peered in to one group and heard her name being mentioned, as well as Kitty's and Sally's. Instantly, Luna knew what they were talking about.

"Guys," Luna whispered, "Word has spread about the investigation, our investigation!"

"Oh no, it was Monique and Hailey wasn't it?" Kitty growled angrily.

"The news has spread *way* too fast!" Sally sighed.

"Well, we still have something against Monique and Hailey, so if she threatens to do anything more then we can just expose her," Eve said with a shrug.

After what seemed like a century of pushing and shoving through other puzzled girls, the five finally reached school. As they entered, they heard the speakers boom, "Eveline, Katerina, Sally, Luna and Megan, report to my office immediately."

It was the familiar voice of their headmistress, Mrs Barrell, and the girls knew that they had been caught in the act. Reluctantly, the girls crawled up to the office and knocked gently.

"Come in," Mrs Barrell said grimly.

The five slowly entered and stood in a semicircle around the room.

"GIRLS! I have heard about this *investigation* concerning Coco's murder and finding out who murdered her. Now, let me make this clear to you. This behaviour is NOT to be tolerated at all at Eveleigh Boarding School for Girls, or anywhere else you go! I know you feel grievance for your lost friend, but that doesn't mean you should be doing something so inappropriate. I thought better of you! As you already know, the police have had the final say and the case is closed.

"Let me make this clear to you. NO MORE INVESTIGATING!" Mrs Barrell boomed. "Understood?"

"Yes, Mrs Barrell," the girls chorused, shuffling around, embarrassed.

"I know how you feel so I'll still let you go to each others' dorms, but if anything – anything – like this happens again, I promise, girls, the permission will be taken off you."

"Yes, Mrs Barrell," the girls chorused again, heading towards the door.

"Now go and head off to dinner. You should be ashamed of yourselves."

And with that, the girls trudged out, truly ashamed of themselves, every one of them.

"Maybe it was for the best…" Luna started.

"Are you kidding? I can't believe you Luna!" Eve exclaimed. "We have to continue, no matter what Mrs Barrell says, remember what Ava said, we have to find a way to make things work!"

Sally, Megan and Kitty were totally confused as they stared from Luna to Eve, and back again.

"Ava this, Ava that!" Luna continued.

The girls stare horrified.

"What? I've just been really stressed lately with this whole investigation thing, and then this happens!"

"We're all stressed, Luna," Megs pats Luna knowingly.

The rest nod and walk off to their own dorms, rather than all staying in one. Just as they were about to sit to do their homework, the dinner bell went.

"Every time! Ugh!" Kitty huffed.

The five trudged down, both physically and emotionally exhausted, grab their food, and sit down around the last table they could see in the dining room. They munched in a painful silence, all worn out for the day. If they were all being honest, they would have rather been in bed sleeping than eating at that very moment.

Tired, they walked all the way back to their dorms, and flopped straight onto their beds.

After hours of twisting and turning, they all decided that it was too hard to sleep that early, and invited Megs and Luna over to their dorm.

"Let's get the suspect list out," Eve said.

Carefully, they took the list out of the drawers and discussed.

"So, we have Hailey, Monique, Jane, Ms. Jacobs, who else?"

"Well, Ava did say we have to put ourselves down right?" Eve remembered.

"But why?" Luna complained. "It's not like we would have a motive or anything. We're her best friends."

"That doesn't matter right now Luna, it's for the safety of our friend," Eve said, and jotted down the names.

"Well at least don't put me down," Luna moaned, "after all, you all know *I'm* her closest friend."

The girls turned and stared, disgusted at Luna.

"Fine, whatever," Luna grumped.

The girls all yawned as they continued writing, until 11:50 at night.

Like dominoes, as Kitty flopped off, so did Eve and Sally, then soon Megs and Luna.

It was lucky too, because Matron was just passing their corridor for her midnight check, and they had all snoozed off, Eve clutching the suspect list in her hand.

Chapter 11

Early the next morning, the girls woke up with a start because of the bright, fluorescent sun beaming through their window.

"One second guys, I need the bathroom so bad!" Luna said.

The girls giggled as Luna rushed out of the room.

Just as the girls finished getting dressed, the breakfast bell went.

"Where's Luna?" Eve asked. "I thought she went to the toilet."

"Oh yes!" Kitty said. "Well, anyways, not to worry, she's not gone forever or anything. Let's just go and eat, the bell has already gone. Anyone coming?"

The girls all agreed and went down just in time to grab two pieces of toast and get the last table in the dining hall. With lots of chatter, they finished their food and were soon getting their books together for their first two lessons. Luna still hadn't appeared.

"Where is that girl?" Megan said.

"I don't know about that, but what I do know is that if we don't get to this PE lesson, Miss Beadle is going to give us extra laps to run."

The girls quickly hurried out, and just as they got to the top floor to cross the building, they noticed Luna and Mrs Barrell at Coco's dorm.

From what the girls had managed to hear, it appeared that Luna had gone in the dormitory and this was obviously forbidden. Luna looked sadly at the girls as she passed by with Mrs Barrell, and the girls waved sadly back too.

As they were crossing from one building to the next, Eve started, "Luna couldn't have – "

"No she wouldn't have - "

"No way!" Megan and Sally chorused.

"No, nada, never - "

"Let's just take that idea out of our minds," Eve sighed.

Contently, the girls continued walking up, until they got to their lesson, and participated, but it was clear that their minds were still on it, from the moment the PE lesson started, to the moment they slept that night.

Next morning, Kitty was already awake as the sun shone so brightly yet again.

"I have so much homework," Sally moaned, as she too started to get up.

"Me too," Eve, Kitty and Megan sighed together.

Luna, however, had no homework to do. She may be mischievous, but she did complete her homework on time, that was for sure.

"Well, I don't have any homework, so I'm just going to see Ava, and maybe stop by at the Chippy in the town centre."

Luna went and got dressed and left just as the breakfast bell went. However, the girls were too distracted to think about breakfast. They were thinking about last night's investigation meeting.

"To be honest, I don't want to do homework right now. We need to continue thinking about Coco. We got too distracted last night," Sally said, looking over at Eve, Eve blushing.

The girls thought hard for at least an hour before Sally realised something.

"Guys! Remember when we were playing 'Truth or Dare' on the coach on the way home from Moroley Avenue?"

"Yes...what about it?"
"Well," Sally continued, "I saw Coco take a sweet out of Luna's jar when they were opposite each other on the coach ride!"

"So?"

"And I thought to just forget about it because Coco was Luna's closest friend, so Coco would only take sweets from her, because remember, Coco doesn't like taking other people's things."

"And?"

"Well, here comes the shocking bit. The sweet was purple."

Eve, Kitty and Megan's jaws dropped.

Sally continued, "And remember Doctor David saying Coco's mouth was purple – "

"– And Luna must have purposely left the purple sweet on the top of the jar because she knew Coco would only take from her stash!" Eva finished.

"Exactly! Wait, how did you know what I was going to say?"

"Oh, Sally," Eve said, "Let's just go and find Luna in the town centre and get her. She probably left us so she could run off without getting caught. I knew Luna wasn't acting herself! We've finally caught out murderer!"

The girls rushed, got dressed into any clothes they could find and rushed out of the building in an instant. They were just in time to see Luna rushing out of 'Ava's Goodies'.

"STOP RIGHT THERE!" Kitty screeched.

"YOU MURDERED OUR FRIEND," Sally raged.

At this point, everyone in the Town Square had gathered to see what was happening.

Luna sneered, "When at last you figured out! I thought you would have figured out sooner, especially you, Eveline! Well, anyways, I'll just be saying my last goodbyes and off I go!"

"CATCH THAT GIRL!" Kitty roared. The whole crowd of people started running in Luna's direction, and eventually, after lots of back and forth motion, Luna couldn't go on anymore, and she stopped at 'Carnivals'.

Meanwhile, the news had spread yet again, and the headmistress had found out and was marching down to 'Carnivals' with what seemed like an army of other teachers.

"Oh, my! I didn't know there were that many teachers in our school!" Kitty muttered.

Miss Beadle hastily called the police to the area and whilst waiting, Mrs Rulebud ties Luna with some rope, and Luna explains to everyone what had happened.

"I'm guessing the question that's all in your heads is: *why*? *Why* would such an obedient girl who does all her homework want to kill one of her closest friends?"

There was a faint mutter from the gathering crowd.

"Well, to spill the tea, here's why. When Coco came to my house one day, she said everything I owned was cheap, and that even my two-bedroom house was cheap and old, and that I should get a new one. I tried convincing her, saying that my parents couldn't afford things now, but she just continued to look down on me. I come from a long line of serial killers, but you never knew, and my parents didn't want to become like them, and they didn't want me to be a serial killer either, but I thought that then was the time to take action, to impress my ancestors and my cousins, as they were always making fun of me for being normal and "too nice".

"So I decided to take illegal food poisoning – purple – and used a syringe to inject it into a sweet and knew she would take it when we were on the coach on the way back from our residential, because we played 'Truth or Dare': and it clearly did its job on her lungs," Luna cackled.

By the time she had finished explaining this, the police had arrived, and Luna was taken away into the police van. It was finally the end of everyone's troubles.

The girls didn't even care to wave goodbye to Luna in the van. Heartbroken and teary, they trudged back to school, leaving the crowd staring in confusion and shock.

Chapter 12

After what seemed like an hour, the girls arrived at school. They took their scarves off reluctantly and went to their dorms. Sally decided to stay with Megan, so she wouldn't be lonely.

"I can't believe it," Megan sniffed, her eyes puffy and her face flushed, "I was sleeping with a murderer this entire time! How can this be? It's been an entire term and I never noticed! No wonder she went to the library all the time, and those dreams I was having of her sneaking out were real!"

"It's alright, we're safe now," Sally sighed.

Eventually, the dinner bell rang and a flood of girls came to queue up in the dining hall. The only thing the four could hear as they passed the corridors was conversation about what had happened in the town centre.

As Eve and Kitty went past, people patted them on the back and cheered for them. When the four met up in the corridor, they hugged each other and continued going down the stairs. On their way, they met Hailey and Monique.

"Well," Hailey sniggered. "Found the murderer? Oh wait, it was LUNA! Amazing! Just brilliant!" Hailey said sarcastically.

"Some kind of friend you had!" Monique said slyly.

Hailey and Monique high-fived and sashayed off. The girls casually ignored them and soon they had got to the dining hall and had collected their food.

As they sat down, Eve said, "At least we found out who did it. We solved a mystery! Our *first* mystery – "

"NO!" Kitty, Megan and Sally said together. The girls all paused for a second, and then started laughing.

After all that had happened that day, the girls were more worn out than they had ever been in their life, and when they got to their dorms, they immediately slept, content and happiness in their minds…

Printed in Great Britain
by Amazon